We Like to Nurse

By Chia Martin

Illustrations by Shukyo Lin Rainey

**Baby monkeys
nurse just like
human babies —
in mommy's arms.**

**Baby elephant nurses
through her mouth
while her trunk
hugs mommy.**

**Mommy spots
and baby spots
blend together to
protect nursing
leopards.**

**Momma giraffe
shelters her baby
on the hot plains
while they nurse.**

**Baby llama nurses
in the cool
mountain breeze.**

**Momma and baby panda
cuddle and nurse
under the bamboo.**

A zebra mommy
munches grass
while her baby
nurses standing up.

**Baby calf drinks
delicious milk from
her mommy.
The more she drinks,
the more mommy makes.**

Piglets wag their tails in delight as they curl up to mommy for lunch.

**Newborn puppies
push against
mommy's nipples
to help the milk
come out.**

**Twin lambs nurse
on either side
of momma.**

**Kittens purr
while they nurse
with momma cat.**

**A newborn colt
nurses with
mommy at sunset.**

We like to nurse.

OTHER TITLES OF INTEREST FROM HOHM PRESS

We Like To Nurse Too
También a Nosotros Nos Gusta Amamantar
by Mary Young
Design by Zachary Parker

This children's picture book focuses attention on our kinship with all mammals, using simple text and delightful full-color illustrations of animal mothers naturally feeding their babies. Children learn about the nursing habits of animals they love from all parts of the world— porpoises, dolphins, sea lions, orca whales and others. This book is the sequel to Hohm Press's highly successful *We Like to Nurse*.

Bi-Lingual ISBN: 978-1-890772-99-4, paper, 32 pages, $9.95; English ISBN: 978-1-890772-98-7, paper, 32 pages, $9.95

Breastfeeding: Your Priceless Gift to Your Baby and Yourself
Amamantar: El Regalo Más Preciado Para Tu Bebé Y Para Tí
by Regina Sara Ryan
and Deborah Auletta, BSN, IBCLC

These inspiring books plead the case for breastfeeding as the healthiest option for both baby and mom. Twenty compelling reasons why "breast is best" are each explained and documented, including recent data that breastmilk feeds the brain in a unique way. More than twenty tender photos demonstrate the beauty and power of the mother-infant bond that is established and strengthened through nursing.

Spanish ISBN: 978-1-890772-57-4, paper, 32 pages, $9,95
English "Easy-Reader" ISBN: 978-1-890772-59-8, paper, 32 pages, $9.95

LIFE SKILLS

Be A GREAT BABYSITTER!

Jim Mack

Heinemann
LIBRARY

www.heinemannlibrary.co.uk
Visit our website to find out more information about Heinemann Library books.

To order:
☎ Phone +44 (0) 1865 888066
📄 Fax +44 (0) 1865 314091
💻 Visit www.heinemannlibrary.co.uk

Heinemann Library is an imprint of Capstone Global Library Limited, a company incorporated in England and Wales having its registered office at 7 Pilgrim Street, London, EC4V 6LB – Registered company number: 6695582

Heinemann is a registered trademark of Pearson Education Limited, under licence to Capstone Global Library Limited

Edited by Pollyanna Poulter
Designed by Philippa Jenkins and Hart MacLeod
Original illustrations © Pearson Education Limited
    by Clare Elsom
Picture research by Elizabeth Alexander and
    Maria Joannou
Production by Alison Parsons
Originated by Modern Age Repro House Ltd
Printed and bound in China by South China
    Printing Company Ltd

ISBN 978 0 431112 40 4 (hardback)
13 12 11 10 09
10 9 8 7 6 5 4 3 2 1

ISBN 978 0 431112 56 5 (paperback)
14 13 12 11 10
10 9 8 7 6 5 4 3 2 1

British Library Cataloguing-in-Publication Data
Mack, Jim
Be a great babysitter! - (Life skills)
649.1'0248
A full catalogue record for this book is available from the British Library.

Acknowledgements
We would like to thank the following for permission to reproduce photographs: © Alamy: pp. **4** (David L. Moore), **14** (Corbis Premium RF/ Colorblind), **22** (Jupiterimages/Comstock Images), **36** (Sally and Richard Greenhill), **38** (Avatra images), **46** (Angela Hampton Picture Library); © Corbis: p. **16** (Michael N. Paras); © Getty Images: pp. **7** (Aurora/Dennis Welsh), **26** (Digital Vision), **43** (Iconica/Camille Tokerud), **49** (Photonica/Betsie Van Der Meer); © Istockphoto: p. **29** (Mike Panic); © Masterfile: pp. **21** (Mark Tomalty), **31** (Chad Johnston), **32** (Tom Feiler); © Pearson Education Ltd: p. **44** (Jules Selmes); © Photolibrary: p. **41** (Hurewitz Creative); © Punchstock: p. **19** (Digital Vision); © Rex Features: p. **12** (Burger/Phanie); © Topham Picturepoint: p. **9** (Bob Daemmrich/The Image Works).

Cover photograph of woman playing with a baby reproduced with permission of © 2008 Masterfile Corporation (Norbert Schäfer).

We would like to thank Kate Madden for her invaluable help in the preparation of this book.

Every effort has been made to contact copyright holders of material reproduced in this book. Any omissions will be rectified in subsequent printings if notice is given to the Publishers.